Dear Parent:
Your child's love of reading starts here!

Every child learns to read in a different way and at his or her own speed. Some go back and forth between reading levels and read favorite books again and again. Others read through each level in order. You can help your young reader improve and become more confident by encouraging his or her own interests and abilities. From books your child reads with you to the first books he or she reads alone, there are I Can Read Books for every stage of reading:

SHARED READING
Basic language, word repetition, and whimsical illustrations, ideal for sharing with your emergent reader

BEGINNING READING
Short sentences, familiar words, and simple concepts for children eager to read on their own

READING WITH HELP
Engaging stories, longer sentences, and language play for developing readers

READING AL~~ONE~~
Complex plots, ch~~aracters, and high-~~ interest topics for the independe~~nt reader~~

D0980681

I Can Read Books have introduced children to the joy of reading since 1957. Featuring award-winning authors and illustrators and a fabulous cast of beloved characters, I Can Read Books set the standard for beginning readers.

A lifetime of discovery begins with the magical words "I Can Read!"

Visit www.icanread.com for information
on enriching your child's reading experience.

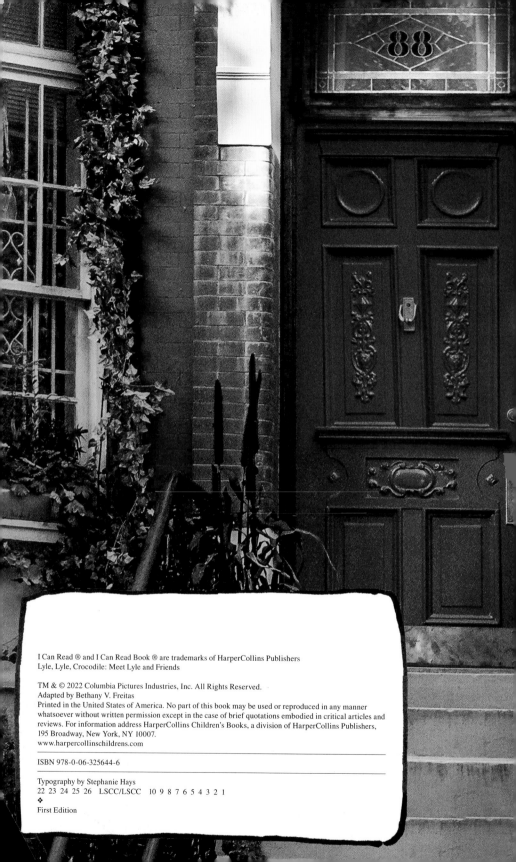

I Can Read ® and I Can Read Book ® are trademarks of HarperCollins Publishers
Lyle, Lyle, Crocodile: Meet Lyle and Friends

TM & © 2022 Columbia Pictures Industries, Inc. All Rights Reserved.
Adapted by Bethany V. Freitas
Printed in the United States of America. No part of this book may be used or reproduced in any manner whatsoever without written permission except in the case of brief quotations embodied in critical articles and reviews. For information address HarperCollins Children's Books, a division of HarperCollins Publishers, 195 Broadway, New York, NY 10007.
www.harpercollinschildrens.com

ISBN 978-0-06-325644-6

Typography by Stephanie Hays
22 23 24 25 26 LSCC/LSCC   10 9 8 7 6 5 4 3 2 1
❖
First Edition

Lyle, Lyle, Crocodile™
Meet Lyle

Based on the Lyle, Lyle, Crocodile books by Bernard Waber

CLARION BOOKS
An Imprint of HarperCollins *Publishers*

CT   2022

This is Lyle, Lyle, Crocodile.

This is the house on East 88th Street.

Lyle lives here with the Primm family.

This is Josh.

Lyle and Josh are best friends.

Lyle showed Josh how to be brave and try new things.

Mrs. Primm is Josh's mother.

She loves having fun with Lyle.

Lyle is part of the family!

13

Mr. Primm is Josh's father.

He was surprised to find

a crocodile living in their house!

But he loves Lyle.

Mr. Grumps lives downstairs
with his cat, Loretta.

Mr. Grumps does not like Lyle.

He doesn't think a crocodile

should live in the house

on East 88th Street.

Before living with the Primms,

Lyle lived with Hector P. Valenti.

Hector loves to perform.

He can sing and dance and do magic!

Lyle loves to sing with Hector.

Lyle is a wonderful singer!

But Lyle is shy.

He doesn't want to perform.

Lyle worries people will be afraid
because he is a crocodile.

But Lyle is not scary.

Lyle is a friendly crocodile!

Josh knows that if Lyle sings, everyone will see how great he is.

With Josh by his side,

Lyle is brave enough to perform.

When they hear him sing,
everyone loves Lyle!

Everyone loves Lyle so much

that he gets to stay

with his family

in the house on East 88th Street.